URGENCY EMERGENCY!
Big Bad Wolf

For Lawrence & Matilda

Library of Congress Cataloging-in-Publication Data

Archer, Dosh, author, illustrator.
[Choking wolf]
Big Bad Wolf / Dosh Archer.
pages cm. — (Urgency emergency!)
First published in Great Britain in 2009 under the title: Choking wolf.
Summary: "A choking wolf is rushed to City Hospital, and
a lost little girl in a red coat has been found, looking for her missing
granny. What on earth did the wolf eat?"—Provided by publisher.
ISBN 978-0-8075-8352-4 (hardback)
[1. Asphyxia—Fiction. 2. Medical care—Fiction. 3. Wolves—Fiction. 4. Animals—
Fiction. 5. Characters in literature—Fiction. 6. Humorous stories.] I. Title.
PZ7.A6727Big 2013
[E]—dc23
2013005440

Printed in China.
10 9 8 7 6 5 4 3 2 1 BP 18 17 16 15 14 13

For more information about Albert Whitman & Company,
visit our web site at www.albertwhitman.com.

URGENCY EMERGENCY!

Big Bad Wolf

Dosh Archer

Albert Whitman & Company
Chicago, Illinois

It was a busy day at City Hospital. Doctor Glenda was writing something important on the wall chart. Nurse Percy was helping someone in a red coat who was crying because she couldn't find her grandma.

Just then the ambulance arrived.

"Urgency Emergency! We have a wolf here who is choking! Choking wolf coming through!"

"Let me examine him," said
Doctor Glenda.

"It's just as I thought—he is choking.
There is something caught in his
throat, which means the air cannot
get to his lungs. We must remove
whatever is stuck in there. Nurse
Percy, I need your help!"

Nurse Percy was hiding under the
bed, shaking with fear.

"He may be a wolf," said Doctor Glenda, "but he is still our patient. He only has minutes to live!

Nurse Percy, can you
overcome your fear of wolves
and help me save him?"

Nurse Percy pulled himself together.
"Good job," said Doctor Glenda.

"Wait," cried Nurse Percy. "What is that noise? Where is it coming from?"

It was coming from
inside Wolf.

"It's more serious than I feared,"
said Doctor Glenda. "It may not
be something stuck in his throat—
it may be some*one*."

She shined a light into Wolf's mouth so she could look down his throat.

"I can see something," she said.
"We must get him or her out."

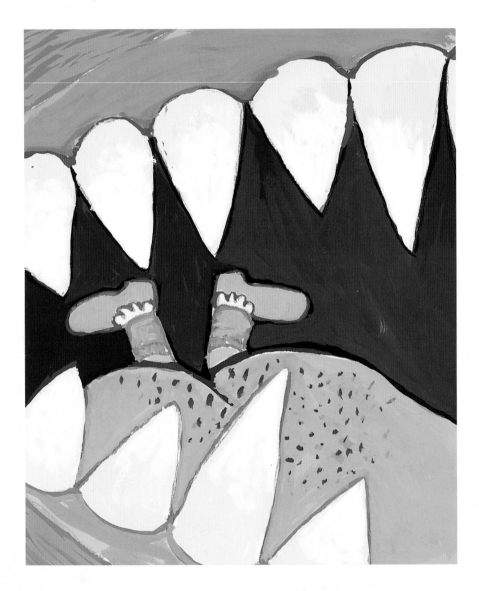

Doctor Glenda slapped Wolf on the back quite hard three times.

Wolf spluttered and gasped,
but nothing happened.

"Nurse Percy," cried Doctor Glenda, "I need your help. I have to stand behind Wolf and squeeze his tummy, so that whoever is down there will pop out."

Nurse Percy made Wolf stand up.

Doctor Glenda reached around his middle and squeezed.

Wolf made weird noises and his eyes seemed to be popping out of his head, but nothing came out of his mouth.

Doctor Glenda tried again.

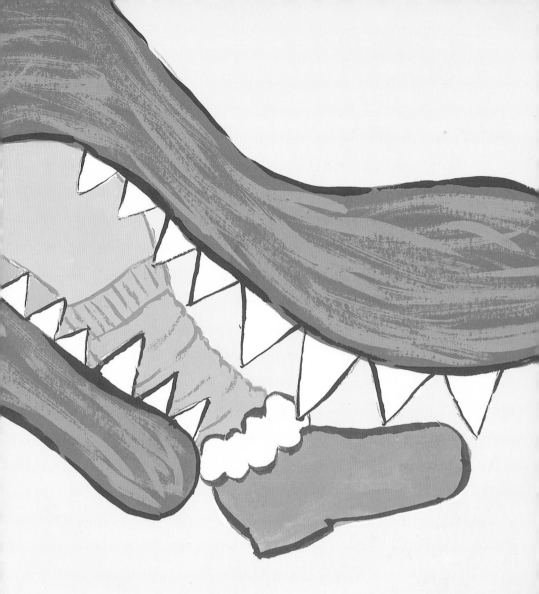

Bleugh! Something poked out of Wolf's mouth.

"It's a pair of slippers!" cried
Nurse Percy. "With someone
wearing them!"

"Once more," said Doctor Glenda.
She squeezed again and out
popped…Grandma!

She was damp and a bit chewed
around the edges, but otherwise OK.

"It's the missing grandma!"
cried Nurse Percy. "Wolf tried to
eat her. That is against the law.
Quick, call the police!"

Wolf tried to escape, but he was too weak from lack of breath to put up much of a fight. Nurse Percy and the team held him down…

...until the police came to take him away.

"I can never thank you enough,"
said Grandma.

"All in a day's work," said Doctor Glenda.

Grandma and her little
granddaughter went off happily.

It was another good job done
by Doctor Glenda and her team.

Enjoy another funny beginning reader in the
URGENCY EMERGENCY! series . . .

ISBN: 978-0-8075-8358-6
$12.99/$14.99 Canada

ALBERT WHITMAN & COMPANY
Publishing children's books since 1919
www.albertwhitman.com